"Swann is a prominent figure in present-day parapsychology. His name is linked with some of the most fascinating laboratory demonstrations of psychokinesis and astral projection. . .Indeed, he is as much the researcher as the researched.

"Ingo is close to unique in his combination of interest and skills. He challenges researchers on their own turf. He is no one's passive 'experimental subject,' but a visionary in his own right. He will surely go on to do and to say things that are novel and provocative; let's watch and listen!"

-- Martin Ebon, *Probe*, November 1975

Ingo Swann (1933-2013) was an American artist and exceptionally successful subject in parapsychology experiments. As a child he spontaneously had numerous paranormal experiences, mostly of the OBE type, the future study of which became a major passion as he matured. In 1970, he began acting as a parapsychology test subject in tightly controlled laboratory settings with numerous scientific researchers. Because of the success of most of these thousands of test trials, major media worldwide often referred, to him as "the scientific psychic." His subsequent research on behalf of American intelligence interests, including that of the CIA, won him top PSI-spy status. His involvement in government research projects required the discovery of innovative approaches toward the actual realizing of subtle human energies. He viewed PSI powers as only parts of the larger spectrum of human sensing systems and was internationally known as an advocate and researcher of the exceptional powers of the human mind.

To learn more about Ingo, his work, art, and other books, please visit: **www.ingoswann.com**.

PURPLE
FABLES
QUARTET

A BIOMIND SUPERPOWERS BOOK
PUBLISHED BY

Swann-Ryder Productions, LLC
www.ingoswann.com

For more information address: www.ingoswann.com.

Previously published in trade paperback by Hampton
Road Publishing Company and Crossroad Press and
digitally by Crossroad Press.

First edition BioMind Superpowers Books.

Cover art: *The God of War Folds His Wings, The God
of Peace Returns* by Ingo Swann © Swann-Ryder
Productions, LLC.

ISBN-13: 978-1-949214-90-1

PURPLE
FABLES

QUARTET

INGO SWANN

To my dear, sweet Mother, Polly,
who read and told me tales
when I was young,
and to John,
who has been so good to her.

Author's Note

ONE MORNING in April 1993, I awoke out of a dream with the title *Purple Fables* spontaneously glowing in my consciousness. I went to the computer and typed it in, and internal whisperings said, "There will be four, a quartet, each of which will be written on four consecutive days." There was the added "instruction" that the draft was not to exceed seventy pages altogether. Then the title "The Temple of Sanity" appeared, and the images of the boy reading the newspaper began dumping his tale into my visualizing mind, *without any premeditation* on my part.

The next morning the second title appeared, "A Clay-Modeling Lesson," although some time ago I'd had a vague idea of this one and had typed out two pages of its content as an insert in something else I was writing. On day three came "The Fate and Destiny of a Travelling Clairvoyant," and on day four, in what amounted to a supreme ecstatic experience, there followed the "dump" of

"Watcher of the Purple River." I say "dump" because it was like turning on a computer and watching it automatically print out something on its own.

I began writing at about 6:30 in the morning and by midday each of the four fables was completed, in four consecutive days. I spent the fifth and part of the sixth day lightly editing them, but they exist in the script mostly as they came out. I decided not to rewrite or intellectually embellish, or even cast them into more acceptable syntax, although some light publishing editing has taken place for this book. Also, on the sixth day I awoke with the Prelude and Postlude which took all of ten minutes to type out, and which I was "told" belonged.

Automatic writing is normally thought of as some kind of psychic dictation. The dictation emanates from a source through the one who is simply writing down what he or she is being told without consciously participating in it. All of the titles I've mentioned above come very close to what we would understand as automatic writing with the distinct sense of psychic dictation. But, somewhat contrasting with the earlier efforts, the purple fables are notable for their economy of presentation, and for the kindly tightness of their mind-image-making sequencing, as well as for the simple symbology.

When I was done, I looked up the meaning of *fable* again. If a fable is a legendary story of supernatural happenings, or a narration intended to enforce a useful truth, then these four *are* fables — not to be confused with fairy tales targeted only for children. These, then, are tales for kind and loving people of all ages.

Some have asked why purple should play an almost magical role in each of the tales. Well, I don't know. Should I have argued with the visions of the title, and superimposed something else instead? I think not, and indeed can see no reason why. If one listens to spirits, why argue with them?

It is generally accepted that colors have symbolic meanings. As to the traditional meanings attributed to the color purple (not to be confused with violet or lavender), in Kabbalistic terms it often refers to "the foundation." The famous theosophical occultist and psychic, C.W. Leadbeater, in his book *Man Visible and Invisible* (1902), gives the meaning as "devotion mixed with affection." J.C. Cooper, in *An Illustrated*

Encyclopedia of Traditional Symbols (1978) gives "royalty, imperial and sacerdotal power, truth, justice, temperance, pomp, and pride." J.E. Cirlot, in his authoritative *A Dictionary of Symbols* (1962) gives "a synthesis representing power, spiritual and sublimation." In ancient alchemy, the legendary and mythical Philosopher's Stone was sometimes portrayed as glowing purple on a white or variegated field.

The fables are, I suppose, mine and not mine — and I'm completely willing to acknowledge their originating, through my own mind-dynamic nets, with other beings or forms of active consciousness within myself. Some who've read the fables in manuscript form, or have read them out loud to others, think that it's my "greater self" speaking. Well, perhaps. I suppose we all have greater selves. My caustic self supposes they exist somewhat hidden among all the intoxications of our lesser selves, so evidently in abundance everywhere, which sell high-impact books and movies as if our appetites for vice, avarice, sex, violence, horror, terror, power, greed, victimization, hatreds, and dissensions were bottomless.

The four purple fables speak with a

kindliness, a softness, an empathy, and with a compassion which is not really characteristic of the sardonic strident sense I more easily recognize in myself. I don't really know how the four purple fables arose or from where they came, and I've no real idea of their literary value or intrinsic meaning in the larger outer scale of things.

Things sometimes come over us — moods, yearnings, visions, raptures; doors open temporarily in consciousness, dump something into our mind, then close; tendrils of passion, perhaps love, compassion, deeper things reach out and grasp us for the magical and transcendent moment. None of this has much explanation, save that it happens, and hardly any of it can be figured into publishers' and sales committees' analyses.

But I do know that inwardly I was dumbfounded, transported, and thrilled almost beyond compare to participate in whatever made, wrote, or dictated the making of these four fables. And approximately twenty-four hours of aesthetic ecstasy is worth it of and in itself.

—Ingo Swann
New York, 1994

Purple Fables

Fables

(Quartet)

CONTENTS

CONTENTS

Prelude

THERE CAME one day to where we are a Sayer of Tales who was hungry and thirsty.

"Take pity on me," said this Sayer, "and feed me for four days, and quench my thirst, for this is the kindly thing to do. And this kindness I'll repay by saying four fables to you, one each in one day.

"And I'll say these fables in ways that let the tales unfold in your minds' eyes — for your usual eyes are bored and tired of seeing only what's out there, and because of this your minds are bored and tired of not working so much."

Now we all are kindly people, and our curiosity and amusement was aroused by this Sayer, hungry and thirsty. And so, for four days we fed that hunger and quenched that thirst.

And then did we watch, one each in one day, four fables said to us, and we watched them unfold in our minds' eyes so that those minds felt better by working at least that little.

The Temple of Sanity

THERE LIVED IN A small neighborhood in a big city a young boy who one day read in a newspaper that the world was an insane place.

Not thinking much about it, he read on and then went about his daily affairs.

But after several days had passed, he found he occasionally thought about this incidental matter, and then began to wonder if it was true or not.

And so he asked his grandmother about it. "Yes, indeed," said she. "I'm very old now. But I've lived through many terrible and insane times, through three wars in which your grandfather and father and elder brother died, and your mother was shot and killed in the street by gangs who snatched her purse — which is why you live now with me. There is crime and trickery and hatred and victims everywhere, much more than earlier in my life.

"And things are getting worse more so and more so, and this is not sanity in the world."

But then the elder woman grew pensive. "You know," she mused, "someone should build a temple of sanity. If I had one last wish before my life ends, I'd like to live to see it."

And there the matter seemed to end, and several years passed until the young boy was becoming a young man. But at times he wished he could show his grandmother the temple of sanity before she died, and so as he grew older he began to wonder what it would look like.

One day he asked her: "Gram, what would the temple of sanity look like?"

Her old eyes lit up with surprise. "Aha, you remember that temple after all these years!"

And so she thought upon this matter, and then said: "Well, I suppose such a temple could be very grand or very simple. Perhaps just a plain room where people could go sit for a few moments and just pretend they were sane. That at least might do them some good."

Now, the elder grandmother owned a small store in the small neighborhood in the big city which sold cheap notions and toys and jewelry displayed against cheap velvet of the color purple hue that faded when in too much light. But these all were cheap things that people felt they could not do without but could not afford if they were too expensive. And the small store sold greeting cards, too, so that people could send their love and admiration to each other whether they meant it or not.

In the back of this store was a small messy room used for storage and boxes and junk. And the young man, who of course by now did most of the work in the shop, decided to clean it out and make a room where his grandmother could occasionally go sit and pretend she was sane.

But when the room was finally cleaned out it looked very barren and empty and didn't look like a temple of sanity at all. So, the young man painted the walls a pleasant color, and festooned it with cheap display velvet of which there was a lot stored here and there, and since the storage room didn't have any windows the purple hue would not fade away so soon. Finally, he found a comfortable soft chair and placed it in the middle of the temple of sanity.

When all of this was accomplished in secrecy he then brought his aging grandmother there and said: "Well, it's not very grand. But since you said that someone should build a temple of sanity so that you could see it before you die, I've decided to be that someone and so I've built this temple of sanity for you to sit in whenever you want."

The grandmother was very moved by this kindly gesture on her behalf, and so she felt obliged to sit in the temple once in a while and pretend she was sane. After sitting there a few times, she began to think she felt better by doing so and smiled more.

But one day she commented that if there were yet another chair in the temple she could invite one or two or her remaining friends alive to sit with her so that pretending she was sane should not be so lonely. The young man then found another comfortable chair, so his grandmother could invite others to sit with her, which they came and did, and all laughed and smiled together while pretending to be sane.

Soon there had to be another chair, and another, and yet another, so that when more came they all would have places to sit and pretend they were sane, a project that brought much happiness and merriment to all of them.

But then came the time when the grandmother began to pass over the end of her bridge of life. But she did not pass along before she called her grandson to her last bedside and said: "You've been a great joy to me, but most of all I thank you for letting me see the temple of sanity before I die."

Of course, when the grandmother was gone forevermore, there was no more need for the temple. But the young man decided to keep it for a while, and then decided to hang a photograph of his elder on the wall, framed in glass, and decorated with ribbons. And much to his surprise, those who had sat with the elder woman soon came and asked if they could sit again, for doing so still made them merry. And so the young man decided that anyone who wanted to could come and sit and pretend they were sane.

But he was now alone in working the store and could not take time to show where the temple was or explain things about it. So he made a small sign that pointed to where the back room was, and then decided to print a small card explaining that anyone who wanted to could sit in the temple and pretend they were sane for a moment or two.

Soon there had to be twelve and then more chairs in the temple, and people began asking where to place their contributions, since their moment of merriment should not go unremunerated. At first, the young man said that pretending sanity should be free to all. But then there was the problem of escalating city taxes that bit deeply into the cheap store's income.

And so, without thinking much about it, he placed a shoe box near the temple's entrance knowing that most people like to pay for what they receive — for then it's really theirs and not someone else's.

After some time had passed, and word had gotten around about the existence of the temple, more came to see it and finally the room was too small, and people began standing in line to get into it. At first only two or three of them, but finally there were so many that the store's usual customers began asking what the line was for. When they found out, they too wanted to see what the temple of sanity was like, and they too began enjoying the merriment of pretending they were sane for a moment or two.

So many began coming that about the only way to cope with all these joyful pretenders was to knock down a wall and make the temple larger. And so this was done, and the now larger room was freshly painted a pleasant color — although so many chairs were now needed that none of them could be very comfortable to economize on space. No one seemed to care, though, and before long this enlarged temple could not yet contain all those who wanted in to it.

Now, there lived in the small neighborhood a press-person who worked for a newspaper in the big city, and who on the way to and from the job noticed the lines waiting to get into the temple — and who of course was curious about what was going on.

Finding out that here was a memorial to an elder grandmother's wish to see a temple of sanity before she died — well, this was a tender human-interest story and subsequently when the newspaper needed a non-news item to place between other more significant news, there appeared a recounting of how the temple of sanity had come to be.

But this little recounting was read by many in the big city and resulted in more people seeking out the temple in the small neighborhood, so they could admire it or laugh at it. And so the lines waiting entrance into it got bigger.

One day someone approached the young man and asked how to become a member of the temple of sanity.

The young man, taken by surprise, didn't know how to answer this, but said that surely sanity was free to all and didn't need memberships.

But then the question of temple membership circulated through the merriment, and many others thought that the temple should have members. And so the young man finally agreed that the temple could have as members any who wanted to be one.

In this way arose the question of membership fees, and what these fees were to be or not required a membership committee to decide. And so the committee on behalf of the temple of sanity came into existence, and thereafter card-carrying members could go to the head of the line and have special access to the merriment of pretending to be sane.

Obviously, by now the temple was not nearly large enough, even with its knocked down wall. And so yet another was knocked down, and a special room had to be arranged so that the committee could sit around a table and decided upon matters.

Among these matters, some committee members felt that the temple should have a more impressive centerpiece than the old grandmother's photograph and circulated a petition to remove it and replace it with something else.

At this the young man finally objected, and firmly so, saying that: "This is my grandmother's temple of sanity, and so it shall remain."

This caused a wave of dissention among the committee, but to little immediate avail when it was realized that the young man owned the premises, and thus the temple, having inherited the store from the last will and testament of the grandmother.

But, as everyone knows, committees have their ways and means of overcoming obstacles by arousing public pressure. The committee clique that wanted to remove the photograph leaked this marginal little story to the neighborhood press-person, and so this little story was then syndicated widely since it was of some unusual interest.

But media-persons need to know what to call things, and so they seized upon some buzzwords trusted to arouse readers' emotional interest and sentimental excitement. Soon the young man found himself being told of in the press as a dictatorial cult-guru leader of an alleged sanity temple that had sprung up behind the scenes in the depths of a small neighborhood — a cult, the news reminded, that was growing in membership.

Naturally, all this media hype focused more attention on the temple. More and more wanted to see it for themselves, and so the lines grew, and then application for memberships, for it was merry to pretend sanity even if dissention rocked the temple itself. Still, though, the guru of sanity would not relent on the issue of the grandmother's photograph, and so there was nothing to be done about it.

And so the photograph-removal-clique gave in, but suggested that additional impressive center-pieces were needed so that the temple members would have something to look at while they were sitting in the temple pretending to be sane.

But the young guru of sanity, again speaking firmly, resisted even this, saying: "Sanity needs nothing to look at, for it is sufficient unto itself."

Some temple members sensed some wisdom in this refusal, and they began to look at the young guru of sanity with different eyes, and began to behold him not merely as a shopkeeper selling greeting cards, but perhaps as someone destined with a mission.

But, as everyone knows, committees have to have something to do to justify their existence. Since it had lost the battle of the elder mother's photograph, it thus had to invent other things that it might do.

And so a new woe soon descended on the young guru's head because the temple committee decided that a very important issue needed to be considered and resolved.

It was this. If the temple of sanity was to be one, then it had to be established what sanity was, and this would determine who would or not be admitted to temple membership. All the committee members agreed that this was a momentous and profound undertaking, but one that would establish the fuller meaning of the temple's existence and give body to its socializing directions.

Naturally, the young guru was aghast, and protested that the temple was just to pretend sanity for as briefly or as long as a person wanted to and so enjoy those moments thereby. But profound issues once born grow in their ways and means, and these issues are always seen to be of higher importance than young gurus are, and so committee discussions began without him.

When intelligence of the nature of the committee's discussions leaked out as it naturally would, many officials in other big-city organizations were irked, since they were accustomed on their parts to deciding what was sanity or not. They agreed in telephone discussions and meetings that surely the upstart sanity cult needed to be investigated and began asking authorities to do so.

And by now there was something to investigate, because the entire greeting-card store had been converted into one big temple of sanity. It had several rooms, and its own printing press which was turning out sanity literature. More walls had been knocked down to provide a lounge where members could relax when they were not seated in the inner sanctum pretending they were sane under the watchful grandmother's eyes in her photograph.

The committee pondering the profound issues regarding what was sanity or not was itself soon convulsed by arguments. Surely, some members argued, it was sane to democratically extend the definition of sanity to include everyone. But others argued that doing so would automatically include those who were insane who should not be admitted to the temple of sanity.

Soon the committee was fractured into two bitterly opposing camps who hurled accusations of excessive liberalism and premeditated fascism at each other.

At this, some temple members resigned and began complaining to investigative reporters that extreme mind-programming efforts were taking place within the temple of sanity, and some even said that it was a danger to society. So soon investigators began infiltrating their agents into the temple of sanity network in an effort to find evidence of this social dangerousness, and speculative stories about the temple were printed far and wide.

By now, hardly anyone believed that the purpose of the temple was just to provide meditative moments for pretending to be sane, and so everyone assumed that this was just a cover-up for more ominous social purposes and direction.

Thus, obvious and covert investigators, squads of media-persons began questioning anyone they could in the small neighborhood in the big city. And so the small neighborhood surrounding the temple itself became alarmed, and began to be concerned for the mental health of their children.

Soon a neighborhood petition, launched by concerned citizens, was circulating to achieve the temple's official removal by legal means — with hints that if legal means were not successful then less legal means might be set afoot.

And, of course, far and wide, even across the nation, many began asking: Just who, exactly, is this young guru of sanity? What is his background? What does he believe? These were questions no one had ever asked before, and so of course no one had any answers.

But since the guru was only a greeting-card merchandiser of cheap jewelry, he actually was no one special, even though he had become the special centerpiece of the temple of sanity. So his devotees felt obliged to invent tales of extra-specialness for him, while his critics likewise felt obliged to invent gossip of his anti-social intentions. And so the guru of sanity was soon referred to by some as inspired, and by others as a minion of dark forces.

How all this might have ended up is hard to say — for in the dark of one night, the temple of sanity collapsed, probably because too many walls had been knocked out to make room for those who wanted to pretend to be sane.

From the ruins the young guru, now getting a little older and perhaps wiser, recovered only his grandmother's photograph, the glass of which was not even cracked.

After haggling about building insurance and expensive reconstruction costs, he rebuilt his greeting-card store, and again sold cheap jewelry and notions people felt they could not live without but could not afford if they were too expensive. He hung his grandmother's photograph in an honored position in the new shop. For a while her image smiled down at him daily until he was shot dead by someone robbing the cheap greeting-card store's cash register and he was then gone forevermore.

After a while, no one in the small neighborhood or in the big city would admit they remembered him or the temple — which is what happens in small neighborhoods in big cities and in other parts of the world, too.

In this way, then, the temple of sanity rose up, and lived for a while, and then fell down — and its former members went their separate ways.

Sanity was never defined.

And so, no one had a special place anymore to go and enjoy the merriment of pretending to be sane — except in the World At Large around them.

A Clay-Modeling Lesson

THE TALE IS TOLD that not too long ago in small poor town in the Middle East, where many mighty civilizations have risen and disappeared, four male babes hardly hours old were found abandoned and left for care. The town's police didn't know what to do with them, and so the four were turned over to social services for lawful disposition.

Now the four babes were remarkable, since they were just exactly alike and obviously sprung from the same one human egg and one seed.

Quadruplets they were, same in all things and manner, and with identical birthmarks on their rears, too. And so some impoverished mother, and father too, had abandoned their four sons — for the land and all was poor and poverty cares not for babes even if they are four alike exactly.

So the poor town's social service people were cast into confusion and alarm. Neither had they seen quadruplets abandoned before, nor did they know where to place them for adoption since all mothers and fathers around already had children of their own, and all were so poor that any more babes would make them poorer still.

So they discussed and argued, these social service people, and days passed and still no one knew what to do. Then it was decided to consult an old man considered wise by many. For when nothing is known of what is to be done, it's best to ask another wiser than all.

Then a social service delegation went to where the wise man lived in a cave when it was cold, and in a hut beside when it was pleasant enough.

And so this old man heard their plight and problem.

"Four babes have been found abandoned," said the delegates, "and in this our town so poor nobody wants them, and something must be done with them. They are remarkable, just alike, and their eyes especially are neither brown nor blue, but of some mixture of both so limpid and deep as to be purple in hue."

At this, the old wise man said: "Then bring these babes before me so that I may see them, and then I'll know what's to be done for them."

So, the delegates trudged hopefully back to town, and made sure the babes were clean and didn't stink and were fed full of artificial milk and dressed and bundled well enough. Then four delegates, one each gently carrying one babe, made their way back to the wise man and before him placed the infants on the ground.

The wise man peered down on them through his watering old eyes. And alike they were, these infants, so much that no one, not even he in his wisdom, knew which was which.

And he saw the infants didn't cry or howl, or even bubble at the mouth, and so he knew they were strong, perhaps even stronger than most, and knew, too, that life anywhere or everywhere would not be too much for them to bear.

So, the wise old man meditated on what was to be done for them, and he breathed in and out for a long silent time while the four social service delegates grew fidgety and bothered at such a long hopeful wait.

Finally, he cleared his throat and said: "The problem is that this is the Middle East, you know, and we know not whether the parents were Moslems or Jews or Christians or what — for all these live in our poor barren land and fight among themselves for who shall be top dog, who shall have what or not, and so they push and shove.

"Into which of these mighty civilizations, then, should these abandoned infants be put? And this is our problem to decide, for we should do best for their unknown parents in giving away their sons into other hands."

And so the four delegates began arguing over this, since one was Moslem, the next Jewish, and the third was Christian. Yet there was one more delegate who was an atheist, and who was already offended because of no mention by the wise man of that cause which pushed and shoved, too.

And so now the real reason was uncovered why there was social service difficulty in disposing of the four babes; for it was now revealed that each delegate thought the infants should be given over to their own push-and-shove persuasion. Thus, the four delegates debated and grew hot with their convictions, all seeking to seize the babes for their own push-and-shove way of living.

Yet, though all this noise, the wise old man drifted into light sleep, for he knew that finally nothing would be decided and then he could speak his piece.

And so it happened, and the delegates grew tired of arguing, and grew hungry, too, and needed to relieve themselves behind nearby rocks, and each hoped that soon all this would be over with so things might return to normal. And perhaps, each thought to themselves, they should decide to do just what the old man recommended, since this was the quickest way to end this affair.

When their arguments were spent, and they all had relieved themselves behind rocks, so they collected again together silently before the old wise man who stroked his old beard and then said: "Since we know not who were the parents, but can conclude that they were either Moslem, Jews, or Christians or atheists, then one child each must be given into families of each persuasion, and then we can be content that we at least decided correctly in one-fourth a way."

At first the four delegates were horrified, or at least pretended to be. But they soon smiled. For here was a solution. And only the wise old man could be blamed for it, not each or even all of them.

"But," the old man continued, "give the infants not into poor families in our poor divided land, for no one here will want them anyway. Send them into nations powerful and strong and rich, for in those nations, too, are Moslems and Jews and Christians and atheists who push and shove to have their own ways."

Now the four delegates nodded in accord, for here was the wisdom they had come to seek. One-fourth a correct solution was better than none, and all knew that rich foreigners would pay heavily for such a strong and remarkable son, and perhaps pay even more through the black-market baby industry.

And sensing that the question of money was now more important than each delegate's convictions, the wise old man grew even wiser when he said: "These babes the four of them are strong, and with inner spirit and fine energies, and so they should have opportunities given them that poor people cannot give.

"Seek out wealthy adoptive parents in the best way you know how, and to each of them and separately give the babes over willingly and without question.

"And in so doing for each, you can rest content that doubtless the unknown parents would again approve if they knew, and this time fully so, for their sons will have what they did not, and will not in future have to abandon their own."

In this way, the four social service delegates knew they had done the right thing by consulting their local source of wisdom, and all was resolved.

And so, as this tale is told, the four brothers were separated and adopted thither and yon and each to different places across oceans and mountains went. And thus, all was done as decided, and many years then passed, and during this passage of time each brother forgot all his others, for babes so young do not remember things such as these.

And during this passage of time, one was brought up a good Christian, and one a good Jew, and another a good Moslem, and the one left over a good atheist.

And since they each were strong and of energy, each grew well and became leaders in their push-and-shove persuasions and ways, and each worked to better those ways as they should and might as if they had truly been born unto them and out of them.

But during this same passage of time, the world was changing and did change in ways unforeseen. And among these changes grew the new idea that the future of humans on Earth could not be as divisive as the past. And since this new idea caught on here and there, growing multitudes began saying that they were frankly tired of so much pushing and shoving ways and began to think of how to give them up.

And so international conferences were set afoot so that those of pushing and shoving ways could sit together for a time without pushing and shoving so much and try to decide how to lessen their differences so that all could be more content.

And so it happened that the four adopted brothers, now long apart and not knowing of each other's existence, were appointed diplomats each to attend one such a conference. Each brother was directed to be a strong and energetic representative to ensure that their four different push-and-shove ways should not give up too much or too little.

Then did the four identical brothers, not knowing they were such, and now of different push-and-shove persuasions, first lay eyes on each other and upon all four together. And they did so at the same time, and they were astonished and confused for none of them knew how they could so exactly resemble each other or why they should.

But there was no mistaking the deep, limpid eyes, neither blue nor brown, but like purple even if not exactly so, eyes each had in common with each other, and eyes they had never seen before anywhere or at any time.

And if their identical eyes, and all identical else about them, did not astonish them enough, then the identical birthmarks on their rears did even more so. And conclusively so that they could not but realize that they all were sprung at the same time from one egg and one seed, for each of them was a sensible man because each had studied science and whatnot in order to become as sensible as possible.

In this way, then, the four were reunited, and all of them together determined to discover how they had been rendered apart. And so their respective families were pressed into confessing all the circumstances of their adoption, even including the name of the poor town in the Middle East where they were found abandoned by parents unknown.

Thither then to this town they went together in anger to discover what they might about their birth, and about why they as quadruplets had been taken each from each other, and then to grow up in different push-and-shove ways, and to live far apart across oceans and mountains.

Once there in that poor town, and since each knew how to push and shove according to their own powerful ways, they questioned and harassed until finally the four social service delegates, now old, told them what they wanted to know.

"It was not our idea," they wailed and cowered. "It was not our decision. We are neither to blame nor are we guilty, since we were at least one-fourth correct, and fully correct in selling you into wealthy families within which and because of which you each have become the fine man you are. And doubtlessly your unknown parents would now be pleased and satisfied."

This confession did not satisfy the brothers, who then asked: "If you are neither guilty nor to blame, then who is? For the decision to separate us unknown to ourselves had to be decided by someone, and we together are very angry at this person. Show that person to us and do so now."

Now the four social service delegates could have lied and said that the wise old man was dead. But they were also now quite afraid of these reunited brothers, strong and energetic, and angry — and who's to know what such anger might inspire?

And so the four delegates confessed that the guilt and blame belonged to the old man who lived outside of town in a cave when it was cold, and in a nearby hut when it was pleasant.

But the four delegates did not say that the old man was a wise one, and that was why they had consulted him in the first place — for the wise are quickly forgotten when their wisdom is not immediately needed.

Thither then to this old man, and immediately so, went the four brothers, and after first getting lost among all the caves and poor huts here and there they finally came upon the old man yet alive and yet older sitting in front of his hut since it was pleasant enough to do so.

Thereupon they vented their complaints and anger on his poor old head and scraggly beard. But he sat calmly, for he too had strength and energy even in his age.

Finally, the four brothers became fatigued with venting their anger, and needed to relieve themselves behind the rocks, and this they did and then returned to the old man.

Then he said: "Sit now down together in front of me where I last saw you as babes bundled clean and not stinking. Let me now look into those same eyes, neither blue nor brown, but of deep and limpid purple strength and energy.

"Let me so look for a while, and then I can tell you if the decision was right."

And so, the four brothers sat promptly down, for they now hoped to learn what they together had come to seek.

And the old man, wise in his ways, regarded them solemnly through his own eyes. He stroked again his scraggly beard, now quite gray and not too clean, for he lived either in a hut or a cave and neither had conveniences even if the world had changed elsewhere.

And he regarded them, each and all four together, until after a while they grew fidgety in the silence drawn out long.

Finally, the old man spoke out: "Know that you each and all four are sprung from the same egg and seed and are therefore not only brothers but identical." The four nodded at this, and then awaited more.

And so the old wise man continued. "But know, too, that one same egg and same seed are sprung from the same human clay out of which all people alive and dead have come and are formed, and out of which those to live and died ahead in time will also have come."

At this, the four brothers frowned. But they were sensible men having studied science and whatnot in order to become such, and so they knew the truth of this. "Speak on, then, old man, but speak clearly, for we are still angry enough."

Thus, the old man spoke on: "Who knows what to do with abandoned babes? And especially so when they are abandoned in a poor town in the Middle East where everyone pushes and shoves, where everyone fights for top-dog status, and where everyone wants to decide who shall have what or not?"

At this, the four brothers did not frown, but nodded well their heads up and down at the same time and in the same way, for they knew of this plight of abandoned children everywhere, each having studied this whatnot also.

But the old man was not done with his speaking, and went on: "Your own eyes told me what to decide on your behalf, for they together showed strength and energy, and each separately too. And so the world needs strength and energy.

"And yet the different peoples of the world drawn out of the same human clay, do they not model that human clay in different push-and-shove ways? And after having done so, then few remember that the clay from which all our eggs and seeds have arisen is the same clay but modeled differently."

At this, and again, the four brothers nodded their heads up and down in exactly the same way and at the same time, and so they began to sense wisdom in this old man.

Still the old man was not done speaking his piece. "Now each of you as human clay and yet identical have been modeled differently. But the result is that between all of you together you possess more together than each of you alone or together would know if you all had been clay-modeled in the same way.

"And so now you know yourselves to be brothers first, and modeled clay second. And with these different kinds of knowledge between you, yet identical from the self-same clay, you can achieve more things than most ever will."

The old man paused, but then went on when he saw the brothers waiting for more. "It was thus to achieve this end, which is not an end but a beginning, considering the way things are in the push-and-shove world around, that I decided to send you into different ways and persuasions fully knowing that each of you clay-modeled differently, yet the same, would one day find your sameness behind your differences.

"For what else is to be done with

abandoned strength and energy when the world must find new ways and means of settling clay-modeled differences, and finding new clay-modeling ways?"

The old man paused again, but only to catch his breath. "And thus you have found your sameness, and now you are here to find why you were clay-modeled differently. And now you know those things.

"And now you know too, that human clay-modeled in anger and push-and-shove forms is of no use either."

At this the four brothers themselves were silent before the old man's wisdom, even if strange. And they were long silent, until the old wise man grew fidgety and felt the need to relieve himself behind the rocks. But the four brothers showed no sign of leaving, since they now wished more to gaze into the old man who they now knew to be wise.

Finally, to get them moving along the old man said: "Get up and go now away from me, and leave me to my hut and my cave. Once you were carried here and carried away as all to be clay-modeled are.

"This time you came on your own feet, and can go again away upon them, and you need none to carry you anymore.

"My decision to send you into the world separately has made you together all wiser, and this combined wisdom you will discover if you talk long about it among yourselves.

"Walk on now, and away from me. Your clay is now yours to remodel together or separately, and you have no more need of me."

And so the four brothers, whose clay was differently modeled yet once again joined, went away, and back they went into the push-and-shove world around. Back into that push-and-shove world where perhaps only four with their wisdom joined are not enough, but perhaps where four are enough for a start, for all clay-modeled things have to start somewhere.

And no one since knows whether the old wise man yet lives, for the wise are forgotten save when they are needed and forgotten even more when few can see the need.

And thus ends the tale of the small poor town in the Middle East where many mighty civilizations have risen and disappeared, and perhaps where they will arise and disappear again.

The Fate and Destiny of a Travelling Clairvoyant

NOT TOO LONG AGO there was born in a backwater place a female child who could see in her mind what was happening on the other side of the mountains, and what was happening across seas and oceans too, and could see also into whatever was hidden.

And she saw all this through some kind of misty purple-hued light, but clearly enough anyway.

She silently amused herself in her infancy by enjoying this seeing within this purple light. And no one knew of this specialness, and even she herself didn't know of it as any special thing so natural it was to her. And so before she knew much at all otherwise, she already knew a lot because of this kind of seeing.

But this female child was born into a time when such seeing was not wanted. And this time was called the Modern Age in which people trusted only in things scientific and had no interest in things otherwise belonging to humans naturally, but which could not yet be made into something scientific.

During this Modern Age, only those of a scientific bent or leaning or understanding were considered really human, and whatever else any other people might be didn't matter.

So, in her early years this child didn't know her specialness was not wanted, and no one, even scientists of the Modern Age, really cared what went on in a backwater place where people are anyway born as they are everywhere else but are generally not scientific enough.

In her childlike ignorance that her special seeing was not wanted in the Modern Age, and as she grew and came to understand words, the child began talking about what she was seeing afar and hidden.

Now, even backwater people can understand some things and backwater places themselves did not belong in the Modern Age. And some backwater people were even proud of this and went about their usual ways whether scientific or not.

And so, too, were they proud of their young female clairvoyant, whom they called a travelling one because, after all, she travelled through the misty purple light and went where they could not.

And so the people of the backwater place in which the child had been born gradually realized that if they wanted to know something all they had to do was ask her about it, and she would tell them of it. But as is not unusual with backwater people, they didn't want to know too much for if they did then life was no longer simple.

And so what they asked this child, now growing up, to see for them concerned matters not too complicated. So, she had only to tell them where lost pigs and cows and children could be found, where important papers had been mislaid, where water was to be found in the ground for new wells, and where septic systems were blocked, and such other things along those lines.

But many in her backwater place thought that her travelling talent would pass and go away as it usually does when first found awakened in children; and they knew, too, that the travelling talent was not wanted in those times, and so they shielded the young girl from outsiders, and sought only to use her talent for their local backwater purposes.

"Yes," they thought and agreed, "the travelling talent would pass, and the young girl would grow up in more usual ways and marry a young backwater boy, and that would be that."

Alas! As the young girl budded and shed her childhood, she became not too pretty. And since young backwater boys lust more after prettiness than not-so-prettiness, no young males could be found who wanted her for other than asking where pretty girls might be obtained.

And, alas again, her travelling talent did not pass and go away even though it misfitted her for living in the Modern Age.

Thus, it transpired that no young

males courted her for herself, which would have interested her and taken up her time, and older males already had their females whom they said they loved.

And so when the girl, passing now into womanhood, was not seeing into local matters, she had a lot of time to kill and decided to interest herself by seeing into all sorts of affairs. Now this small backwater place had a newspaper published once a week, and usually its poor two pages were filled to the brim with local gossip and want ads and advertisements for farm equipment and building supplies, and notices about what was lawful fishing and hunting or not.

But occasionally someone wrote about what was going in the world beyond the backwater place, and so one day the young woman volunteered to write about what she saw was to come out of those world matters since this would give her something to do when there was nothing else for her to do.

But by now in her growing up, the young woman understood what interested backwater people the most, and so she started up her writing by saying when tornados would come, and where they would, and when the river would flood, for those in whom this travelling talent are awakened can see into the future, too.

And since what she said this way came to pass, and her seeings helped people get out of the way of these disasters, then there was for a time more demand for her talent in other ways and directions.

Now, sometimes backwater people are not very smart, but sometimes they are not too stupid either.

And so some few began to worry that if their travelling clairvoyant could see all that she did, then perhaps she could see also into certain of their wrong-doing secrets that had best not be seen into.

"Yes," they thought among themselves, "this seeing woman needs a man by now, for then she would stay busy enough seeing after him and not into their secret affairs!" And so there was renewed effort to find one for her.

Still no man wanted her yet, and some even said they were now afraid of her. And besides, some of these men protested, what man would want a woman who could easily see into what he did all of the time?

So, even if it was well and good that this clairvoyant woman could see into what the locals wanted her to and help them get out of the way of tragedies, still there was the matter of her seeing into what of their wrong-doings they did not want sighted.

So something now had to be done to rid the backwater place of this clairvoyant in order to preserve its secrets and its usual ways and its peace.

Now, as is not unusual when people don't know what to do, they go and consult someone else about it.

There lived not too far from this backwater place a minister of the flocks that still came to be ministered to — although not very many did by now, since this was the Modern Age time, and ministering in his ways was not considered scientific enough. Yet since there was no one else to ask about this seeing matter, he was asked about it, but only informally so.

"Well," this minister said after he

thought he had grasped the matter according to his understanding, "the first thing to do is to seek out whether this seeing is of heaven or hell."

Here is a weighty and profound matter, for neither heaven nor hell should be taken lightly.

And since these profound matters both are discussed in the Bible, a copy of which everyone in the backwater had whether they actually read it or not, so the pages of this good and mighty book were opened here and there.

And sure as shoot, some were able to perceive that this type of seeing was of hell.

But the travelling clairvoyant herself had a copy of the Bible, and she had earlier read its mighty pages not just here and there, but the whole Good Book many times.

And so she pointed out Proverbs 27:12 which says: "A prudent man foreseeth the evil, and hideth himself; but the simple pass on, and are punished."

Now, this added fuel to the smoldering fire, for the Good Book itself said that those who did not like this kind of seeing were simple people.

And in this way in the backwater came the bother of the question of who was simple or not, for all those that did not want seeing into their secrets obviously were among the simple who would pass on into the punishment that might otherwise be avoided if they tolerated foreseeing in the first place.

Here, then, was both a rock and a hard place, and many in the backwater place found themselves in between.

Now, as things go in the whole world as well as in its backwaters, secrets usually take precedence over foresightful prudence.

And so since clairvoyants can see into the former and sometimes provide the latter, perhaps it is best that their seeing talents pass and go away before they cause troubles to arise between secrets and prudence.

In any event, such troubles had now arisen in the backwater place, and its usual ways were disrupted, and that place was not any longer in peace. And no one knew what to do about their travelling clairvoyant — save to bum her up as a minion of hell as in the days of old, but which was no longer legally possible in the Modern Age.

Now, the backwater clairvoyant was, after all, a clairvoyant, and so she could see that her time and place in the backwater were ended. And thus, to the joy of most of those backwater peoples, they awoke one day to find she had removed to some other place they knew not where.

And few could care, and men, and women, too, could stand about again without threat of their secrets being known.

Now they had to find their lost pigs and cows and children the best they could and tear up their whole septic systems to find only one block in them, and many expensive drillings again had to be put into the earth to find just one well with water. And when tornados and floods now came, they came once more with unforewarned surprise, and people as before had to quickly scramble out of their way if there was time enough to do so.

Now removed from the backwater place, the travelling clairvoyant travelled both in body and mind until she reached a new place where no one was because no one else had ever wanted it but was pleasant enough to stay.

Once there at this empty but pleasant place, she determined to do something that had never been done before, save in ancient days.

"Here," she determined to herself, "should be built a place where clairvoyants, young and old and in between, should come to study their travelling seeing talents and develop them more fully, so that prudent people can indeed ask what might be foreseen as they should."

Since she was one such clairvoyant, she foresaw how to raise sufficient money, and did so immediately, and then built up that pleasant place so that it could contain the many to come.

And so, when this new place was learned of here and there, some few came at first, and others sent some few of their children in whom the seeing talents seemed to dwell, since the parents thought that these precious indwelling talents should be awakened further and that they should be strengthened so that they should not later pass and go away.

And so then some few more came to this new place of seeing development, and then some few more, until there were more than just a few altogether, for many are they that are born with the seeing talents, and perhaps all have them without knowing so, and where were they to go if not to such a place as this new one.

In this way, the Great Seeing Project had begun, carefully guided by the seeing woman from the backwater place. And it no longer mattered to anyone if she was pretty or not, and in any event, she now needed no man to fill her time since there was always much for her to do and oversee.

But this was yet in the times of the Modern Age in which such seeing was not wanted, and as the Project grew in size and population, it also grew in implications.

And shortly alarm arose here and there and even far and wide.

This alarm arose because, as in the backwaters, the bearers of the Modern Age had many wrong-doing secrets, too, that none of them wanted to have seen into — secrets that such a many developing seers might see into, and even foresee outcomes of them that could not be prudently now kept hidden, even if the simple passed on in front of those secrets and then suffered because they did not know of them.

And this alarm arose, too, because Modern Age science had derided such seeing talents, and had declared them non-existent. And so scientists knew nothing of them, for how could they if they thought they were non-existent?

And certainly, it would be true that if such talents did exist, then science could be accused of not being scientific enough to have investigated them before.

So now here was a new problem for the clairvoyant, fled from a backwater, who had now removed herself and her great work to a new place, and yet had entered into a same problem only on a larger scale.

So she said to herself: "Well, the place may be different, but the problem is the same.

"People everywhere have secrets they do not want seen into, and so seeing talents are not wanted anywhere even if people naturally have them anyway.

"And so too will this new place be put down, and this I foresee, too."

And so the clairvoyant grew pensive in her thinking and behavior — which was understood by young and old and in between clairvoyants working in the Project since they could see into her thoughts as well was as into anyone's.

Finally, she gathered together all in the Project and told them that they, all of them, were in a race against time, for their undoing was heading their way.

And now this undoing did head their way, for Modern Age science, so guilty of denying the travelling seeing talents, now had to keep this denial secret, and felt justified in so doing since any other way would end up in opening everywhere all secrets to inspection by those who possessed enough travelling clairvoyance to see into them.

Now science could hardly fall back on the argument that such seeing was of heaven or hell since this self-same science held the Good Book in disrepute as a worthless superstitious document.

But science has ways and means of getting things accomplished, and its methods are even easier. All that needed to be done was to declare something unscientific to be done with it, since no one in the Modern Age dared go into anything so declared.

And so it was told about that the

Great Seeing Project was unscientific, which is the same as saying that it was of hell.

And so this was quickly done, and without much fuss. And then those that might have come to the new place to study and develop their travelling seeing talents began questioning their own talent in the light of whether it was scientific or not. In this way, then, confusion was aroused, and when in confusion people go to others to help straighten it out.

And so those confused went for answers to where they might go if all things were honest and equal — to science itself to find out if their talents were scientific or not.

Now, as has already been told, science itself knew nothing of whether such talents were scientific or not. The reason for this was that earlier scientists at the beginning of the Modern Age had said such talents did not exist in the first place. And so what does not exist cannot be made scientific. Thus, even though science knew nothing at all of such seeing talents, it knew enough, it thought, to say that they were unscientific.

And what is unscientific should never be given a gain-hold in society, lest society fall out of the control of science itself, and so the Modern Age had taught that what was unscientific was also a danger to everyone.

Now, as all things go, people generally do not like what they are told is dangerous to them, and become much disturbed at any such prospect.

And so, before long the Great Seeing Project was surrounded by protesters carrying placards, while that same Great Seeing Project found itself within the media guns of investigative reporters.

And so that place, empty and pleasant enough at first, was now encumbered with so many that one had hardly enough room to breathe, and the grounds around were beaten into dust and littered with vast amounts of soda pop cans and beer cans left by those who sought to refresh themselves while protesting.

At this, the clairvoyant and her seeing students inside this siege had to come to terms with themselves.

And so, it was realized that the travelling seeing talents were not wanted anywhere, and not in this Modern Age time.

Then the seeress spoke to those around her, for she had finally seen something she knew she should have seen all along but had not: "Alas," she said, "the time is not ripe for us. The time yet has not come for people everywhere to realize they can see as we do.

"And so, if we are to live we must do so secretly, for if anything is to live in these present times it must do so largely by secret ways and means.

"This is the ultimate working wisdom of the world out there, which is false, which is not our way. But even so we must go forth from this place cloaked in it and stay so cloaked until the time is come when people realize that they need to see and foresee what will befall them unless they do so see and foresee."

And this cloaking all the seers took upon themselves, young and old and with ages in between, and they took the Great Seeing Project with them to some other place no one now knows where. Thus, did world affairs return to normal, and go as is usual everywhere.

And then the prudent people again could not foresee the evil and avoid it, and the simple again passed on and are still punished for their simpleness as the great and Good Book warned.

And since then when children find themselves possessed of the awakened travelling clairvoyance, everyone is content to let that talent return to sleep and pass and go away.

For if it does not then upsets and trouble come their way.

Such, then, is the fate and destiny of a travelling clairvoyant until the Modern

Age has come and gone, and other times come and arrive.

The Watcher of the Purple River

HERE AND THERE in very out-of-the-way places beyond where life is only the usual and where science yet knows not, a tale is sometimes told of a very old woman who was thought to be crazy and too much touched by the Moon and magic and things like that. That she was very old cannot be denied, for her shriveled skin hung down and crinkled, and her old eyes had become pinpoints of less-than-focused gazing as if she no longer saw what was what or saw anything at all.

At least four generations of passers-by each had said they had seen her yet alive in their times. And some who passed by even remembered that their grandmothers had said that their own grandmothers, and then earlier grandmothers, had known of her, too.

So, many wondered if she were far

beyond her time and perhaps should have gone on into eternity long ago.

So, no one living now knew how old was this very old woman, and she seemed to live on although everyone else died.

Yet, to the confusion of all who saw her, she moved sprightly and dressed well, though plainly. And she vigorously tended her gardens of vegetables and flowers, and these she often gave to those who passed by and said a kindly hello.

And then here was yet another mystery, for her gardens grew well, and animals from nearby woods did not come into them and eat what they wanted, and insects seemed to go to other places to suck and chew. And neither did her plants suffer such things as root rot and brown leaf curl.

Not so many passing by did say that hello to her, though, for she was likely to say: "Well, the currents of death are collecting around you, and have gripped you, and so you should see to your affairs and make the will," or something like that —or something else that no one really wanted to hear just because they said hello to her.

And here was yet another mystery, for what she said was to come did come sooner or later and usually sooner.

And because of so many mysteries in one place and around one old woman, the only way to explain them all was to call the woman crazy, although this explained nothing from the start.

Now, this very old woman, with her vegetables and flowers that grew in abundance, lived in a small house on the bank of a very wide river big and deep.

And so big and so deep it was that its by-flowing waters were dark enough to seem of the color purple hue.

And so it was called the Purple River by one and all, and this from a time that no one now remembered.

And when the old woman was not seen tending her gardens, she was often then seen gazing into these by-flowing purple waters as if there were something to be seen in them besides the water flowing along.

And this gazing she did so long and

so often that people thought she was crazy more and more to look at water this way, even if it were purple colored, and if even flowing by. For there was nothing different to be seen because it just flowed along all the time and in the same way.

One day, though, while the old woman was thus watching the Purple River, a naked young man was seen swimming downstream in it and he hailed the woman and asked for help because he had somewhere fallen in and was drowning.

But the old woman just shrugged her shoulders and hailed back at him: "Well, you're drowning because you're swimming the wrong way. If you swim downriver with the currents, then they will take you where they want, and then there is nothing more to say."

Thank goodness for the naked young man, some men were passing along the Purple River's bank, and as most will do they made haste to give a hand and get him out and save his life.

And after that the young man was not in very good shape and needed to rest on the bank to gather his wits and his life energies back together into one working thing.

And not knowing what else to do for him, the saving men then went along their way, and left the young man with the crazy old woman to tend.

And they left quickly enough so that they would not have to hear from her something they did not want to hear.

And so the old woman studied the naked young man carefully while he gathered his wits and such, and saw everything about him in great detail, and when she had seen all she wanted of his frontside, she told him to turn over so she could see his backside, too.

And when she had finished all this looking, she pursed her aged old lips and thought for a time.

Then she finally said to him: "Well, the Purple River has brought you here to me for a reason, and if you want to stay here with me for a while I'll tell you what it is.

"But this reason cannot be told in only a few moments, or even only overnight. So you must stay a longer while to find that reason out."

Hearing the old woman thus speak at him, the naked young man felt interest in him stirring about what this reason might be, for he didn't know why he had fallen into the Purple River in the first place.

Yet in it he suddenly was, and by no known action of his own, and then the purple waters were all around and their flowing currents taking him where they wanted.

And so he said that he would stay, and then the old woman found him some old clothes left over from some bygone husband or another. And she fed him from her garden and sat him out among her flowers so that he could take some kind of healing from their beauty.

Thus, his wits and his energies quickly came back into one piece as they should, for he was young and his door into eternity yet someplace far distant and ahead.

When all this was done, the old woman began her sayings to him.

"Can you see," she asked, "that Purple River yonder over there, that selfsame one that brought you here and in great distress?"

And he said that of course he could see it, for any fool could see it there as well as he.

And so she asked him to tell her what he saw, and he said he saw the river wide and deep and flowing by.

"But what else can you see?" asked the old woman smiling in her aged way.

"But what else is there to been seen of that river?" the young man asked. "For that the river's wide and deep and flowing by is all that is to be seen."

"Well, for one thing," the old woman now said, and merrily so, "you have not told me of what is flowing within the river, for there is much within it to be seen as well."

But at this the young man protested, for he said that no one could see into the waters, and that it was illogical for anyone to think otherwise.

"But you are using only your eyes," giggled the old woman, "and this as most do, and so they see only what the eyes can see."

Since there was some logic to this,

the young man sat silently, and the old woman then continued. "Now listen carefully and understand that what the eyes can see is only what they are designed to see.

"And although this at first seems like everything seen by them is all that there is to see, yet the eyes see only what they do of all things to be seen, and this is really very little of what exists that is to be seen.

"And so any who see only what the eyes can see actually see very little of what is to be seen."

And she went on, this old woman: "Now again listen carefully, and understand that all and each and everyone have many ways of seeing what is to be seen beyond what the eyes can. And understand too that you have these different ways. Just ask each cell in your body what they can see, and all will speak in unison into your mind that they see much more altogether than what the eyes can."

Now the young man knew that more existed than what his eyes could see, and so he had no reason to protest these sayings, and so he waited for the old woman to go on.

And go on she did. "From this chair in which you are sitting among these my beautiful flowers, go by these other ways of seeing, and go now into the depths of the Purple River and stand deep within those depths for a time, and walk around until you have therein seen enough and all that you want, and then tell me what you have thus seen by these other ways of seeing."

And so the young man closed his eyes, so that he would not see only what they saw, and soon he found himself seeing in the deep waters, although by ways he did not know how.

And there he saw many things. Some beautiful such as the bottom river plants, and then some things foul, too.

And then he saw the fishes, and marked their different kinds, and saw that these were swimming against the deep river's currents in order to keep their place where they wanted.

And so he also saw then some old beer cans here and there and other junk as well, and rubber tires from somewhere embedded in the river rocks and sands.

And there too he saw three old cars

rusting and wrecked, and in one of these he saw an old satchel filled with a good amount of money, although quite soaked and slimy.

And when he had enough of such seeing, he then told the old woman what he saw deep in the Purple River by these other ways of seeing.

And when he had told her thus, she then went on again and said: "Now, we must resolve whether you saw what you did or not, so that you can understand more fully that you have these many other ways of seeing what's what.

"So go now from among my beautiful flowers and find those very same saving men who pulled you to me from the river, and say to them that those old car wrecks are there, and say too that I'm tired of seeing them when I look out and over and into that Purple River.

"But be sure to tell them too of the slimy soaked money hidden in one of them! Be sure to tell them that it is there, and that it will belong to any who finds it!

"Be sure to tell them this one thing,

for they will not otherwise come along."

So the young man left his comfortable place among her beautiful flowers and did what the old woman had bid him to do. And then soon with the young man there came floating down the Purple River a big old sledge barge equipped with an old rusting hoist with cables and hooks for dragging up things from deep within water, and this barge was steered by those same saving men now intent on pulling up that soggy money from its hiding place.

And so all this was done soon enough, and the saving men went happily on their way, although arguing how to split the slimy money among them. And they took away with them on the barge those old wrecks so that the old crazy woman would not have to see them anymore in the depths of the Purple River. And this, she thought, was best for the Purple River's ecology, too.

"Now, then," asked the old woman of the young man, "know you that you have seen what you have by these other ways of seeing?" And he said that he now knew that, even though he was very amazed and shaken.

The very next day, seated again among her beautiful flowers, the woman said to him: "Now I will begin telling you more of the reason that the Purple River brought you to me, and know that this reason is to learn what is to be told to you by me."

And so the young man sat silently and attentively, and readied his body and mind cells to listen also.

"See you that Purple River yonder over there," the old woman asked, and when the young man nodded that he did she went on: "That Purple River is very wide and deep, and so wide that it is difficult to see the distant banks even if there is no fog hanging about.

"Well, listen now and understand that there is another river akin to it, and it too is very wide and deep.

"This is the River of Life, although it

is very much wider and very much deeper, and even so very wide that few ever see its very distant shores, even if the fogs of life are not hanging around."

And she then continued: "Now listen again and understand then that what the eyes see of this River of Life is actually very little of it. Yet even so there are in this other river many things just as there are in the Purple River.

"In this River of Life are things beautiful and foul, and wrecks of life, too, and the junk of life left over from it and befouling its river ecology.

"And there are life currents going where they want, and if you cannot see them well enough to swim against them, like the fishes in the Purple River do, and keep your place in all these currents flowing, then these self-same life currents will take you where they want, and then there is nothing more to say about what happens to you or about where you end up.

"Now know and understand that the eyes alone cannot see any of these things, and so you must use your other ways and means so as to see them enough."

When the old woman was done saying, and now resting from so much of it, the young man thought over all her saying, and then finally asked: "But how is one to see such things, and by what different seeing ways and means?"

"Well," responded the old woman, "do you ask your eyes how they see what they do?

"Do ask you ears how they hear what they do?

"Now listen and understand that most people have no idea at all how their eyes see or how their ears hear, and even if they do know anything of these matters, still their eyes anyway see and their ears hear, and do whether those matters are understood or not.

"And so eyes see what they do, and it may be that no one knows how they so see, but they anyway see what they see.

"These other ways and means of seeing are no different, and they too see what they do whether you know not how they do, and they see into the depths of the River of Life equally as they see into the depths of the Purple River."

And so the young man was again

silent, but the old woman went on anyway: "Now listen and understand that you must show yourself these other ways and means of seeing, and so I will take you into my gardens and show you some things."

And then she went into her gardens, and the young man followed where she went.

And she went on through her gardens until she came upon some seeds awaiting planting. "Here," she then said, "are some seeds awaiting their entrance into the River of Life.

"Your eyes see only how they look all alike — although some are larger, and some are smaller, as any eyes can see.

"But some are good seeds and will grow well, and others may not grow too well, and some of these seeds are bad ones, and will not grow very much if at all.

"Take you now all these seeds together and separate them according to whether they are good or bad ones, or in between ones, and make your separations according to your other ways and means of seeing."

And so the young man began the task, tedious at first, of separating those many seeds of which the eyes could see that they only looked alike — although some where larger or smaller than others.

And after a long time had passed he finally had three piles of seeds, and the old woman said that they would now plant them in three separate rows not too far apart, and thus they would eventually see how the young man's separating of them had worked, and this would take many days and weeks.

The next day the old woman began again. "Regard these my gardens well now and take as long as you want to do so."

And so the young man regarded these — which didn't take very long, for hers were small gardens yet not too small.

After this garden overlooking, then the old woman went on: "Know and understand that these my gardens are wonderful and healthy, and then wonder why the animals of the nearby woods do not come in the night to eat of them what they want.

"And wonder why these my plants do not suffer from root rot or brown leaf curl, and why insects that might suck and chew on them too go elsewhere to suck and chew in the gardens of others."

And so the young man wondered as he was bidden to do, but he could see nothing of why all this was so.

So the old woman then said: "Well, then ask your other ways and means of seeing to show you what they can."

And she then awaited him to do so, and after a while he said that he thought he saw an imaginary leopard stalking in the gardens here and there and stalking carefully enough to avoid stepping on the plants growing wonderful and healthy.

"Yes!" smiled the old woman. "I've created that my leopard from within my mind and asked him to patrol these my plants, and please to take care not to stomp on them while doing so.

"And some such thing as this goes on within the River of Life, which itself is filled with such things imagined by others whether they know so or not, and such things are set adrift the River of Life's currents where they latch on to whatever they can.

"But the animals in those woods yonder and nearby can see these imagined things for they haven't yet learned that they should use only their eyes to see, and then see only what their eyes can see.

"But not yet having learned this as humans have so learned, the animals there can see my leopard and so of course will not come into my gardens to eat of them what they want. And this, too, is part of what goes on in the River of Life."

At this, the young man was astonished and very much so, and even more so astonished when the old woman's mind-created leopard itself realized that the young man was mind-seeing it in this way, and so came and sniffed and purred at the young man's legs, for the old woman had mind-created a kindly leopard and not a fierce one.

And so he saw, too, and by these his new seeing ways and means, that the old woman had mind-created a fine big net of blue and twinkling lights over her gardens, and so the sucking insects had to go fly or crawl to other gardens and suck and chew of those plants they found there. And with so much mind-energies here and there over her gardens, root rot and brown leaf curl decided not to rot and curl in her gardens.

In this way, then, did the young man begin to see into the River of Life, and see also that in this river many things were there to be seen.

And he began to understand the reason he had been cast up out of the Purple River at the feet of the old woman.

And more, he began to understand understanding also, and knew that one should see what there is to be seen, and so see by all ways and means possible. And to accomplish this manifold seeing before making up any understanding.

And after some time had passed

again, finally the three rows of his separated seeds sprouted and grew enough so that the proof of his separation of the seeds could now be seen.

And so it was then seen that the best seeds he had selected from all the others then did grow the best, while the bad seeds didn't grow at all or very little. And so he now knew that it would have been best not to have planted and tended those bad seeds in the first place.

And so he learned now much from the old woman, but it was she who yet had not taught him enough.

And so she continued: "Listen and understand that many bad seeds are planted in the River of Life, and even as are bad things thrown into the Purple River and sometimes come to rest in that river where it irks me to have to see them there when I look across and over and into the currents flowing in that Purple River.

"And in that River of Life are its own flowing currents, and if you cannot see them by any means possible, then you are cast into that river helplessly.

"And so the currents will take you where they want, whether this be among beautiful or foul things therein it.

"And remember, too, that in that River of Life are those mind-created things set loose in it, like old wrecks, and these old life wrecks catch up unsuspecting people if they drift aimlessly in the currents."

And so the young man now understood this too, for it was not really very hard to understand, and he now knew that the River of Life had invisible things in it, and its own currents, too.

And after he had time to so understand, the old woman now said: "Now we must exercise your new-found ways and means of seeing so that you can know them better.

"Go and bring those saving men to me so that I can thank them for lifting out those old car wrecks so that I don't have to see them anymore deep within the Purple River.

"But when you come up to them, now then use your other ways and means of seeing to see where those saving men are at in the currents of the River of Life — see whether they are swimming against the currents and thus maintaining their place in that River of Life, or whether they are adrift within its currents and going with those currents to where they know not, whether it ultimately will be among what is beautiful or foul.

"And look too at them to see what mind-imagined things have latched onto them and see whether these are beautiful or foul."

And so again the young man went to do as the old woman bid him to do. And soon again there came back with him the gaggle of saving men, but better dressed now from finding their treasure in the Purple River.

And so the old woman thanked them for grappling into the Purple River's depths and taking away the old car wrecks so that she need not see them anymore.

But through all these thanks was watching the young man, and he saw that one of those saving men was not swimming against the currents in the

River of Life, but was surrounded by things foul in that river, and was ill from latched-on imaginings, although that saving man knew it not yet.

And so the young man said to this saving man: "Well, I see that the currents of death are collecting around you, and so you should see to your affairs and make the will."

At this, the old woman smiled knowingly, and nodded her head with approval. And the young man had spoken so because he now knew that the River of Life had downward-dragging currents of death in it that catch unknowing people in them and take them into their eternity elsewhere.

But the saving men rolled their eyes, for now there were two crazy people to avoid here on the bank of the Purple River. And even though these saving men said they appreciated the old woman's thanks, they did now depart quickly enough before one or another of them heard another thing not wanted to be heard.

But since it was because of her they had become rich enough to buy their new clothes, they really should have thanked her instead of she thanking them, and yet such too goes on in the River of Life.

Now all this took place on the bank of the Purple River, and still the old woman said more to the young man about what goes flowing by and within the River of Life.

She said this and that, and when he had understood, she said this and that more, until he finally had learned enough about those this-and-thats to serve him well.

But when all this understanding was accomplished, the young man said back to her: "Well, you're now old and I'm young, and so I have to begin thinking of all this in ways more appropriate to us who are young."

And so the old woman asked: "So how then would you think of these things about the River of Life which itself is far older than I and you and everyone added together ever will be?"

So now the young man taught the old woman, and this is as it should occasionally be, but not always so. "Well, listen and understand, then," he said, "that the River of Life has its ecology, and this ecology can be beautiful or fouled, and it can be one or the other or not.

"But this ecology is surely to be fouled up if people cannot see all of that river they should and can.

"For everyone does have these other ways and means of seeing into that river, and if they don't use those ways to see what they might, then the downward flowing currents of the River of Life will catch them up and do what they want with such people, and then there is nothing more to say about it."

At this, the old woman smiled, and seemed herself to grow younger for a moment.

But she thought to herself that it was best to let this young man see those Life-River ecological things as if he were the first to see them precisely thus and so. For even though she had seen them that way all along, the young need to know themselves independently of the old and aged.

"So then," feigning ignorance of the River of Life's ecology, she said back to the young man: "I too have learned something new. And I've learned it from you, and I am glad enough to learn it."

And the young man himself now smiled and even seemed to grow younger again, although he had no immediate need of that.

Now the old woman spoke again: "And so then the reason the Purple River belched you up at my feet, even if saving men helped, is now understood both between us and of us separately."

And so it was.

The young man stayed on for a time, doing exercises to strengthen his new ways of seeing. But the time was finally over with, and as is with all the young they have their own things to go and do.

And so the old woman and the young man embraced for a long time, and then for some more longer time, for age between them no longer mattered, as it does not matter in the River of Life itself.

But after embracing was done, the young must head into that river, for the young are already and always in it whether they know not or know not how.

Yet the old must go another way into that river and into eternity somewhere since it is into that eternity that the River of Life empties itself, and both this old woman and this young man knew this bittersweet fact of the River of Life.

Taking his departure, then, the young man said: "I shall go as I came, naked, and into the Purple River."

And so he took off the clothes left over from some one of the old woman's husbands or another, and plunged back into the purple waters flowing by.

But this time he swam against the currents, and headed upstream, and easily changed his place among the flowing currents when need be, and he paused only long enough to wave a naked arm and hail back to the old woman a friendly hello.

When the young man was thus gone, and in this way, the old woman felt herself contented, and when not tending to her vegetables and flowers she again watched out over the Purple River.

And she was once more contented to see that the old rusting car wrecks were nowhere to be seen, at least right in front of her.

And what else was there for her to do before she empties into eternity, this crazy woman, too touched by the Moon and by magic, and so avoided by many because she said to them things they did not want to hear?

Yet her mind-imagined leopard said hello to her every day and sniffed and purred at her legs.

And perhaps this is enough hellos for any one day, and such too goes on in the River of Life, even in that out-of-the-way place by the Purple River few have ever heard of and thus never come there to watch it flow by.

Postlude

AND SO WE LISTENED to these tales told to us by that Sayer of Tales, and who told us one tale in each of four days.

And each time that we listened we watched the tales also unfold in our minds' eyes, and these then felt better for working at least that little.

And so we told the Sayer that we would feed any more hunger and quench any more thirst, and do so to have more tales told.

But the Sayer of Tales said: "I can't stay. There are places to go and things to see. But your own minds' eyes can see their own tales if you let them — and can see more than tales if you let them also."

A BioMind Superpowers Book from
Swann-Ryder Productions, LLC

www.ingoswann.com

OTHER BOOKS BY INGO SWANN

Everybody's Guide to Natural ESP
Master of Harmlessness
Penetration
Penetration: Special Edition Updated
Preserving the Psychic Child
Psychic Literacy
Psychic Sexuality
Reality Boxes
Resurrecting the Mysterious
Secrets of Power, Volume 1
Secrets of Power, Volume 2
Star Fire
The Great Apparitions of Mary
The Windy Song
The Wisdom Category
Your Nostradamus Factor

Printed in the USA
CPSIA information can be obtained
at www.ICGtesting.com
LVHW091502010924
789859LV00007B/126

9 781949 214901